# Dear Parents:

Congratulations! Your child is taking the first steps on an exciting journey. The destination? Independent reading!

**STEP INTO READING**® will help your child get there. The program offers five steps to reading success. Each step includes fun stories and colorful art or photographs. In addition to original fiction and books with favorite characters, there are Step into Reading Non-Fiction Readers, Phonics Readers and Boxed Sets, Sticker Readers, and Comic Readers—a complete literacy program with something to interest every child.

## Learning to Read, Step by Step!

### Ready to Read   Preschool–Kindergarten
• big type and easy words • rhyme and rhythm • picture clues
For children who know the alphabet and are eager to begin reading.

### Reading with Help   Preschool–Grade 1
• basic vocabulary • short sentences • simple stories
For children who recognize familiar words and sound out new words with help.

### Reading on Your Own   Grades 1–3
• engaging characters • easy-to-follow plots • popular topics
For children who are ready to read on their own.

### Reading Paragraphs   Grades 2–3
• challenging vocabulary • short paragraphs • exciting stories
For newly independent readers who read simple sentences with confidence.

### Ready for Chapters   Grades 2–4
• chapters • longer paragraphs • full-color art
For children who want to take the plunge into chapter books but still like colorful pictures.

**STEP INTO READING**® is designed to give every child a successful reading experience. The grade levels are only guides; children will progress through the steps at their own speed, developing confidence in their reading. The F&P Text Level on the back cover serves as another tool to help you choose the right book for your child.

Remember, a lifetime love of reading starts with a single step!

To Mr. Haley, Mrs. Duncan, Mr. Keane,
and Mr. Moore. Thank you.
—F.G.

To Ms. Carrillo, for making kindergarten
such a delight
—E.U.

Text copyright © 2022 by Frances Gilbert
Cover art and interior illustrations copyright © 2022 by Eren Unten

All rights reserved. Published in the United States by Random House Children's Books, a division of Penguin Random House LLC, New York.

Step into Reading, Random House, and the Random House colophon are registered trademarks of Penguin Random House LLC.

Visit us on the Web!
StepIntoReading.com
rhcbooks.com

Educators and librarians, for a variety of teaching tools, visit us at RHTeachersLibrarians.com

*Library of Congress Cataloging-in-Publication Data*
Names: Gilbert, Frances, author. | Unten, Eren Blanquet, illustrator.
Title: I love my teacher! / by Frances Gilbert ; illustrated by Eren Unten.
Description: First edition. | New York : Random House Children's Books, 2022. |
Series: Step into reading. Step 1 | Audience: Ages 4–6. | Audience: Grades K–1. |
Summary: A girl loves her teacher and loves going to school so much that at home she plays teacher to her pets.
Identifiers: LCCN 2021014805 | ISBN 978-0-593-43052-1 (trade paperback) |
ISBN 978-0-593-43053-8 (library binding) | ISBN 978-0-593-43054-5 (ebook)
Subjects: LCSH: Teachers—Juvenile fiction. | Schools—Juvenile fiction. |
CYAC: Teachers—Fiction. | Schools—Fiction.
Classification: LCC PZ7.1.G547 Iai 2022 | DDC 813.6 [E]—dc23

Printed in the United States of America
10 9 8 7 6 5 4 3 2 1
First Edition

This book has been officially leveled by using the F&P Text Level Gradient™ Leveling System.

STEP INTO READING®

STEP 1 READY TO READ

# I Love My Teacher!

by Frances Gilbert
illustrated by Eren Unten

Random House 🏠 New York

I have my backpack.

I have my coat.

I have my lunch.

I am ready to go
to school!

I say goodbye to
my dog

and my cat

and my hamster.

"I will see you
after school!"

My teacher waits outside the school to say hello.

Some kids shake hands.

Some kids wave.

I give my teacher a
high five.

I put my backpack
and my coat
and my lunch
in my cubby.

We start our day
with circle time!
We sing our
morning song.

We talk about the
days of the week.

There is so much
to learn!
My teacher
teaches me
how to read.

My teacher
teaches me
how to write.

My teacher
teaches me
how to count.

My teacher
teaches me
how to paint.

# My teacher teaches me how to tell time.

I love school!

After school,
it is my turn
to be the teacher.

I say hello
to my class.

I shake hands
with my dog.

I wave to my cat.

I give my hamster
a high five.

I teach my class
how to read
and write.

I teach my class
how to count
and paint.

# I teach my class
# how to tell time.

I am a good teacher!

But my teacher
is the best teacher.

And tomorrow
I get to see her again!

# I love my teacher!